Belle Etoile

Heureux

Petit-Soleil

Cheri

BEAUTY
AND THE BEAST

•

PRINCESS BELLE-ETOILE

•

THE YELLOW
DWARF

With 21 color plates

WALTER CRANE
BEAUTY AND THE BEAST
AND OTHER TALES

Introduction
by Anthony Crane

THAMES AND HUDSON

AND THE METROPOLITAN MUSEUM OF ART

© 1982 Thames and Hudson Ltd, London
Introduction © 1982 Anthony Crane

First published in the USA in 1982 by Thames and Hudson Inc.,
500 Fifth Avenue, New York, New York 10110

Library of Congress Catalog Card Number 82-80982

ISBN 0-87099-303-8 (Metropolitan Museum)
ISBN 0-500-01285-7 (Thames and Hudson)

Printed and bound in Portugal by Gris

INTRODUCTION

THE STORIES IN THIS BOOK are classics which have given pleasure to millions of children at least since the 17th and 18th centuries when they were devised or refurbished by French authors. One of them, *Beauty and the Beast*, has remained a familiar favourite, but it is high time we were able to visit again the parts of fairyland described in *The Yellow Dwarf* and *Princess Belle-Etoile*. And for our guide we have Walter Crane, whose pictures make them magic.

Walter Crane had a photographic memory particularly for objects and animals, and, as he did not rely on models or notebooks in the way many other artists did, he was able to adapt and refine familiar things seen or recalled to produce effects so much more fascinating than reality.

It was no more difficult for him to draw a richly attired 'Beast' than any other person or creature, although he was in some doubt about putting cloven hoofs on his arms; in one of the set of coloured designs for this book – hanging on the wall of the room in which I write – he has given him a dramatically upraised hand as he discovers Beauty's father picking the rose, while still delineating wholly appropriate boots to accommodate the cloven hoofs on his legs.

His rather serious Victorian critics would sometimes take Walter Crane to task on matters of this kind. With his usual confidence and ability to draw 'out of his head' he had painted his 'Swan Maidens' as one of a number of allegorical and symbolic pictures. He was criticised on their anatomy and proportions, and for not having used a model. His reply was that neither he nor anyone else had actually seen a Swan Maiden, so it was difficult to draw one accurately from life!

Even when he used in his illustrations furniture in his own home, such as the sofa on which Beauty and the Beast sit, it is suitably transformed and enhanced for its decorative purpose. The outdoor scenes in this story, with the château and formal gardens, clearly derive from France. In *Princess Belle-Etoile* the influence is Italian, with orange trees, and boats invented from what he had seen in Venice a few years before when he had stayed with his newly married wife in a palazzo on the Grand Canal.

Orange trees figure even more prominently in *The Yellow Dwarf*, for it was in one of these that the dwarf was supposed to reside. Again, in spite of its lion, the landscape is Italian, as is the tiled court. These pictures also provide examples of Walter Crane's dauntless ability to suspend disbelief – in the graceful portrayal of swans as draught animals and the even more improbable but temporarily convincing transformation of a cat into a steed.

Walter Crane's involvement with children's books came about in a natural and almost inevitable way. His father, Thomas, himself a painter, portraitist and lithographer, was not materially successful, although he was exhibiting at the Royal Academy towards the end of his life. So when he died at the age of 51 after years of poor health, the family was left in poverty.

One of the last things Thomas did before he died was to apprentice Walter (then only 13) to the wood-engraver William James Linton. It was in this same year, 1859, that Thomas died and in the following year Walter was able to contribute to the family fortune a wage of ten shillings a week, which he earned until his discharge in January 1862. The young Walter had put his name in a firm but unformed hand to an undertaking that 'the said Apprentice his Master faithfully shall serve, his secrets keep and his lawful commands obey'. When he left, the indenture was returned annotated: 'Returned with thanks and full expression of satisfaction at Walter Crane's thorough good conduct, his readiness, his industry and his ability.'

He was not apprenticed to learn engraving but the quite separate and important craft of drawing on the wood, then an essential stage of the progress from original design to printed page. He describes how it was done: his teacher 'set me down at his table to draw one of my own pen-and-ink sketches on a small block of boxwood, showing me the way to prepare it with a little zinc-white powder (oxide of bismuth was generally used) mixed with water and rubbed backwards and forwards on the smooth surface of the boxwood until dry. On this the design was traced in outline and then drawn with a hard pencil to get the lines as clear and sharp as possible for the engravers. I did not find the 4H pencil put into my hands a very sympathetic implement, though the surface of the wood was pleasant, but I dashed off something with it. . . .'

After he had completed his apprenticeship small commissions came his way, initially from Linton's, and soon from Edmund Evans, first for railway novels, and then children's books or 'toy books'. Walter Crane continued to draw his own designs on the actual block until 1871, the year of his marriage and his protracted stay in Rome. By that time it had become possible to photograph the key outline direct on to wood from drawings made on card. These could go easily by post and Walter Crane continued to work on his toy books while he was in Italy. Apart from not having to handle the blocks his method of procedure remained the same.

He would work out the designs in pencil, trying out different variations of composition (I have at least three sketches for some of the pages of *The Yellow Dwarf*). When he was satisfied he would produce one or more full-colour finished drawings, trace the outlines and transfer them to the block, or the card when the photographic method was used, and prepare the finished outline drawing. Edmund Evans' engravers then cut the block. Walter Crane would be sent black and white proofs, which he would colour and return to Edmund Evans, who then had separate blocks made for each colour required. Of course colours could be overprinted to give a wider range, but even so 5 or 6 different blocks and printings would be required.

Walter Crane insisted on regarding toy books such as these as a sideline, essentially belonging to the days of his youth. These three were done in 1874 and 1875 by the time he was 30, and the last one – *The Sleeping Beauty* – came out in 1876. It is true that they formed only a comparatively small part of his vast range of work. This merely reflects his great creativity and commitment as a designer, both in head and heart. His professionalism provided a common channel for his emotions, as is shown by the equal care and enthusiasm he put into the designs for his fancy-dress parties and the gravestone for one of his infant children.

In these pages the intention is to divert and delight; nothing would please my grandfather more than to feel you were sharing the fun he tells us he got out of designing them.

ANTHONY CRANE

BEAUTY and The BEAST

WALTER CRANE'S TOY BOOKS

A B C

SHILLING SERIES

: LONDON & NEW YORK :
GEORGE · ROUTLEDGE
AND · SONS

BEAUTY AND THE BEAST.

ONCE upon a time a rich Merchant, meeting with heavy losses, had to retire to a small cottage, with his three daughters. The two elder grumbled at this; but the youngest, named Beauty, tried to comfort her father and make his home happy. Once, when he was going on a journey, to try to mend his fortunes, the girls came to wish him good-bye; the two elder told him to bring them some nice presents on his return, but Beauty merely begged of him to bring her a rose. When the Merchant was on his way back he saw some fine roses, and thinking of Beauty, plucked the prettiest he could find. He had no sooner taken it than he saw a hideous Beast, armed with a deadly weapon. This fierce-looking creature asked him how he dared to touch his flowers, and talked of putting him to death. The Merchant pleaded that he only took the rose to please his daughter Beauty, who had begged of him to get her one.

On this, the Beast said gruffly, "Well, I will not take your life, if you will bring one of your daughters here to die in your stead. She must come willingly, or I will not have her. You

may stay and rest in my palace until to-morrow." Although the Merchant found an excellent supper laid for him, he could not eat; nor could he sleep, although everything was made ready for his comfort. The next morning he set out on a handsome horse, provided by the Beast.

When he came near his house his children came out to greet him. But seeing the sadness of his face, and his eyes filled with tears, they asked the cause of his trouble. Giving Beauty the rose, he told her all. The two elder sisters laid all the blame on Beauty; but his sons, who had come from the forest to meet him, declared that they would go to the Beast instead. But Beauty said that as she was the cause of this misfortune, she alone must suffer for it, and was quite willing to go; and, in spite of the entreaties of her brothers, who loved her dearly, she set out with her father, to the secret joy of her two envious sisters.

When they arrived at the palace the doors opened of themselves; sweet music was heard, and they walked into a room where supper was prepared. Just as they had eaten their supper, the Beast entered, and said in a mild tone, " Beauty, did you come here willingly to die in place of your father?" "Willingly," she answered, with a trembling voice. "So much the better for you," said the Beast; "your father

can stay here to-night, but must go home on the following morning." Beauty tried to cheer her father, at parting, by saying that she would try to soften the heart of the Beast, and get him to let her return home soon. After he was gone, she went into a fine room, on the door of which was written, in letters of gold, "Beauty's Room;" and lying on the table was a portrait of herself, under which were these words: "Beauty is Queen here; all things will obey her." All her meals were served to the sound of music, and at supper-time the Beast, drawing the curtains aside, would walk in, and talk so pleasantly that she soon lost much of her fear of him. At last, he turned towards her, and said, "Am I so very ugly?" "Yes, indeed you are," replied Beauty, "but then you are so kind that I don't mind your looks." "Will you marry me, then?" asked he. Beauty, looking away, said, "Pray don't ask me." He then bade her "Good-night" with a sad voice, and she retired to her bed-chamber.

The palace was full of galleries and apartments, containing the most beautiful works of art. In one room was a cage filled with rare birds. Not far from this room she saw a numerous troop of monkeys of all sizes. They advanced to meet her, making her low bows. Beauty was much pleased with them, and said she would like some of them to follow her and keep her company. Instantly two tall young apes, in court dresses, advanced, and placed themselves with great gravity beside her, and two sprightly little monkeys took up her train as pages. From this time the monkeys always waited upon her with all the attention and respect that officers of a royal household are accustomed to pay to queens.

Beauty was now, in fact, quite the Queen of the palace, and all her wishes were gratified; but, excepting at supper-time, she was always alone; the Beast then appeared, and behaved so agreeably that she liked him more and more. But to his question, " Beauty, will you marry me?" he never could get any other answer than a shake of the head from her, on which he always took his leave very sadly.

Although Beauty had everything she could wish for she was not happy, as she could not forget her father, and brothers, and sisters. At last, one evening, she begged so hard of the Beast to let her go home that he agreed to her wish, on her promising not to stay away longer than two months, and gave her a ring, telling her to place it on her dressing-table whenever she desired to go or to return; and then showed her where to find suitable clothes, as well as presents to take home. The poor Beast was more

sad than ever. She tried to cheer him, saying, " Beauty will soon return," but nothing seemed to comfort him. Beauty then went to her room, and before retiring to rest she took care to place the ring on the dressing-table. When she awoke next morning, what was her joy at finding herself in her father's house, with the gifts and clothes from the palace at her bed-side.

At first she wondered where she was ; but she soon heard the voice of her father, and, rushing out, she flung her arms round his neck. The father and daughter had much to say to each other. Beauty related all that had happened to her at the palace. Her father, enriched by the liberality of the Beast, had left his old house, and now lived in a very large city, and her sisters were engaged to be married to young men of good family.

When she had passed some weeks with her family, Beauty found that her sisters, who were secretly vexed at her good fortune, still looked upon her as a rival, and treated her with coldness. Besides this, she remembered her promise to the Beast, and resolved to return to him. But her father and brothers begged her to stay a day or two longer, and she could not resist their entreaties. But one night she dreamed that the poor Beast was lying dead in the palace garden ; she awoke in a fright,

looked for her ring, and placed it on the table. In the morning she was at the Palace again, but the Beast was nowhere to be found : at last she ran to the place in the garden that she had dreamed about, and there, sure enough, the poor Beast was, lying senseless on his back.

At this sight Beauty wept and reproached herself for having caused his death. She ran to a fountain and sprinkled his face with water. The Beast opened his eyes, and as soon as he could speak, he said, sorrowfully, " Now that I see you once more, I die contented." " No, no!" she cried, "you shall not die! Oh, live to be my husband, and Beauty will be your faithful wife!" The moment she had uttered these words, a dazzling light shone everywhere; the Palace windows glittered with lamps, and music was heard around. To her great wonder, a handsome young Prince stood before her, who said that her words had broken the spell of a magician, by which he had been doomed to wear the form of a Beast, until a beautiful girl should love him in spite of his ugliness. The grateful Prince now claimed Beauty as his wife. The Merchant was soon informed of his daughter's good fortune, and the Prince was married to Beauty on the following day.

PRINCESS BELLE-ETOILE.

ONCE upon a time there were three Princesses, named Roussette, Brunette, and Blondine, who lived in retirement with their mother, a Princess who had lost all her former grandeur. One day an old woman called and asked for a dinner, as this Princess was an excellent cook. After the meal was over, the old woman, who was a fairy, promised that their kindness should be rewarded, and immediately disappeared.

Shortly after, the King came that way, with his brother and the Lord Admiral. They were all so struck with the beauty of the three Princesses, that the King married the youngest, Blondine, his brother married Brunette, and the Lord Admiral married Roussette.

The good Fairy, who had brought all this about, also caused the young Queen Blondine to have three lovely children, two boys and a girl, out of whose hair fell fine jewels. Each had a brilliant star on the forehead, and a rich chain of gold around the neck. At the same time Brunette, her sister, gave birth to a handsome boy. Now the young Queen and Brunette were much attached to each other, but Roussette was jealous of both, and the old Queen, the King's mother, hated them. Brunette died soon after the birth of her son, and the King was absent on a warlike expedition, so Roussette joined the wicked old Queen in forming plans to injure Blondine. They ordered Feintise, the old Queen's waiting-woman, to strangle the Queen's three children and the son of Princess Brunette, and bury them secretly. But as she was about to execute this wicked order, she was so struck by their beauty, and the appearance of the sparkling stars on their foreheads, that she shrank from the deed.

So she had a boat brought round to the beach, and put the four babes, with some strings of jewels, into a cradle, which she placed in the boat, and then set it adrift. The boat was soon far out at sea. The waves rose, the rain poured in torrents, and the thunder roared. Feintise could not doubt that the boat would be swamped, and felt relieved by the thought that the poor little innocents would perish, for she would otherwise always be haunted by

the fear that something would occur to betray the share she had had in their preservation.

But the good Fairy protected them, and after floating at sea for seven days they were picked up by a Corsair. He was so struck by their beauty that he altered his course, and took them home to his wife, who had no children. She was transported with joy when he placed them in her hands. They admired together the wonderful stars, the chains of gold that could not be taken off their necks, and their long ringlets. Much greater was the woman's astonishment when she combed them, for at every instant there rolled out of their hair pearls, rubies, diamonds, and emeralds. She told her husband of it, who was not less surprised than herself.

"I am very tired," said he, "of a Corsair's life, and if the locks of those little children continue to supply us with such treasures, I will give up roaming the seas." The Corsair's wife, whose name was Corsine, was enchanted at this, and loved the four infants so much the more for it. She named the Princess, Belle-Etoile, her eldest brother,. Petit-Soleil, the second, Heureux, and the son of Brunette, Cheri.

As they grew older, the Corsair applied himself seriously to their education, as he felt convinced there was some great mystery attached to their birth.

The Corsair and his wife had never told the story of the four children, who passed for their own. They were exceedingly united, but Prince Cheri entertained for Princess Belle-Etoile a greater affection than the other two. The moment she expressed a wish for anything, he would attempt even impossibilities to gratify her.

One day Belle-Etoile overheard the Corsair and his wife talking. "When I fell in with them," said the Corsair, "I saw nothing that could give me any idea of their birth." "I suspect," said Corsine, "that Cheri is not their brother, he has neither star nor neck-chain." Belle-Etoile immediately ran and told this to the three Princes, who resolved to speak to the Corsair and his wife, and ask them to let them set out to discover the secret of their birth. After some remonstrance they gained their consent. A beautiful vessel was prepared, and the young Princess and the three Princes set out. They determined to sail to the very spot where the Corsair had found them, and made preparations for a grand sacrifice to the fairies, for their protection and guidance. They were about to immolate a turtle-dove, but the Princess saved its life, and let it fly. At this moment a syren issued from the water, and said, "Cease your anxiety, let your vessel go where it will; land where it stops." The vessel now sailed more quickly. Suddenly they came in sight

of a city so beautiful that they were anxious their vessel should enter the port. Their wishes were accomplished; they landed, and the shore in a moment was crowded with people, who had observed the magnificence of their ship. They ran and told the King the news, and as the grand terrace of the Palace looked out upon the sea-shore, he speedily repaired thither. The Princes, hearing the people say, "There is the King," looked up, and made a profound obeisance. He looked earnestly at them, and was as much charmed by the Princess's beauty, as by the handsome mien of the young Princes. He ordered his equerry to offer them his protection, and everything that they might require.

The King was so interested about these four children, that he went into the chamber of the Queen, his mother, to tell her of the wonderful stars which shone upon their foreheads, and everything that he admired in them. She was thunderstruck at it, and was terribly afraid that Feintise had betrayed her, and sent her secretary to enquire about them. What he told her of their ages confirmed her suspicions. She sent for Feintise, and threatened to kill her. Feintise, half dead with terror, confessed all; but promised, if she spared her, that she would still find means to do away with them. The Queen was appeased; and, indeed, old Feintise did all she could for her own sake. Taking a guitar, she went and sat down opposite the Princess's window, and sang a song which Belle-Etoile thought so pretty that she invited her into her chamber. "My fair child," said Feintise, "Heaven has made you very lovely, but you yet want one thing—the dancing-water. If I had possessed it, you would not have seen a white hair upon my head, nor a wrinkle on my face. Alas! I knew this secret too late; my charms had already faded." "But where shall I find this dancing-water?" asked Belle-Etoile. "It is in the luminous forest," said Feintise. "You have three brothers; does not any one of them love you sufficiently to go and fetch some?" "My brothers all love me," said the Princess, "but there is one of them who would not refuse me anything." The perfidious old woman retired, delighted at having been so successful. The Princes, returning from the chase, found Belle-Etoile engrossed by the advice of Feintise. Her anxiety about it was so apparent, that Cheri, who thought of nothing but pleasing her, soon found out the cause of it, and, in spite of her entreaties, he mounted his white horse, and set out in search of the dancing-water. When supper-time arrived, and the Princess did not see her brother Cheri, she could neither eat nor drink; and desired he might be sought for everywhere, and sent messengers to find him and bring him back.

Princess Belle-Etoile.

The wicked Feintise was very anxious to know the result of her advice; and when she heard that Cheri had already set out, she was delighted, and reported to the Queen-Mother all that had passed. "I admit, Madam," said she, "that I can no longer doubt that they are the same four children: but one of the Princes is already gone to seek the dancing-water, and will no doubt perish in the attempt, and I shall find similar means to do away with all of them."

The plan she had adopted with regard to Prince Cheri was one of the most certain, for the dancing-water was not easily to be obtained; it was so notorious from the misfortunes which occurred to all who sought it, that every one knew the road to it. He was eight days without taking any repose but in the woods. At the end of this period he began to suffer very much from the heat; but it was not the heat of the sun, and he did not know the cause of it, until from the top of a mountain he perceived the luminous forest; all the trees were burning without being consumed, and casting out flames to such a distance that the country around was a dry desert.

At this terrible scene he descended, and more than once gave himself up for lost. As he approached this great fire he was ready to die with thirst; and perceiving a spring falling into a marble basin, he alighted from his horse, approached it, and stooped to take up some water in the little golden vase which he had brought with him, when he saw a turtle-dove drowning in the fountain. Cheri took pity on it, and saved it. "My Lord Cheri," she said, "I am not ungrateful; I can guide you to the dancing-water, which, without me, you could never obtain, as it rises in the middle of the forest, and can only be reached by going underground." The Dove then flew away, and summoned a number of foxes, badgers, moles, snails, ants, and all sorts of creatures that burrow in the earth. Cheri got off his horse at the entrance of the subterranean passage they made for him, and groped his way after the kind Dove, which safely conducted him to the fountain. The Prince filled his golden vase; and returned the same way he came.

He found Belle-Etoile sorrowfully seated under some trees, but when she saw him she was so pleased that she scarcely knew how to welcome him.

Old Feintise learned from her spies that Cheri had returned, and that the Princess, having washed her face with the dancing-water, had become more lovely than ever. Finding this, she lost no time in artfully making the Princess sigh for the wonderful singing-apple. Prince Cheri again found her unhappy, and again found out the cause, and once more set out on his white horse, leaving a letter for Belle-Etoile.

In the meanwhile, the King did not forget the lovely children, and reproached them for never going to the Palace. They excused themselves by saying that their brother's absence prevented them.

Prince Cheri at break of day perceived a handsome young man, from whom he learned where the singing-apple was to be found: but after travelling some time without seeing any sign of it, he saw a poor turtle-dove fall at his feet almost dead. He took pity on it, and restored it, when it said, "Good-day, handsome Cheri, you are destined to save my life, and I to do you signal service. You are come to seek for the singing-apple: it is guarded by a terrible dragon." The Dove then led him to a place where he found a suit of armour, all of glass: and by her advice he put it on, and boldly went to meet the dragon. The two-headed monster came bounding along, fire issuing from his throat; but when he saw his alarming figure multiplied in the Prince's mirrors he was frightened in his turn. He stopped, and looking fiercely at the Prince, apparently laden with dragons, he took flight and threw himself into a deep chasm. The Prince then found the tree, which was surrounded with human bones, and breaking off an apple, prepared to return to the Princess. She had never slept during his absence, and ran to meet him eagerly.

When the wicked Feintise heard the sweet singing of the apple, her grief was excessive, for instead of doing harm to these lovely children, she only did them good by her perfidious counsels. She allowed some days to pass by without showing herself; and then once more made the Princess unhappy by saying that the dancing-water and the singing-apple were useless without the little green bird that tells everything.

Cheri again set out, and after some trouble learnt that this bird was to be found on the top of a frightful rock, in a frozen climate. At length, at dawn of day, he perceived the rock, which was very high and very steep, and upon the summit of it was the bird, speaking like an oracle, telling wonderful things. He thought that with a little dexterity it would be easy to catch it, for it seemed very tame. He got off his horse, and climbed up very quietly. He was so close to the green bird that he thought he could lay hands on it, when suddenly the rock opened and he fell into a spacious hall, and became as motionless as a statue; he could neither stir, nor utter a complaint at his deplorable situation. Three hundred knights, who had made the same attempt, were in the same state. To look at each other was the only thing permitted them.

The time seemed so long to Belle-Etoile, and still no signs of her beloved

Cheri, that she fell dangerously ill; and in the hopes of curing her, Petit-Soleil resolved to seek him.

But he too was swallowed up by the rock and fell into the great hall. The first person he saw was Cheri, but he could not speak to him; and Prince Heureux, following soon after, met with the same fate as the other two.

When Feintise was aware that the third Prince was gone, she was exceedingly delighted at the success of her plan; and when Belle-Etoile, inconsolable at finding not one of her brothers return, reproached herself for their loss, and resolved to follow them, she was quite overjoyed.

The Princess was disguised as a cavalier, but had no other armour than her helmet. She was dreadfully cold as she drew near the rock, but seeing a turtle-dove lying on the snow, she took it up, warmed it, and restored it to life: and the dove reviving, gaily said, " I know you, in spite of your disguise; follow my advice: when you arrive at the rock, remain at the bottom and begin to sing the sweetest song you know; the green bird will listen to you; you must then pretend to go to sleep; when it sees me, it will come down to peck me, and at that moment you will be able to seize it."

All this fell out as the Dove foretold. The green bird begged for liberty. " First," said Belle-Etoile, " I wish that thou wouldst restore my three brothers to me."

" Under my left wing there is a red feather," said the bird: " pull it out, and touch the rock with it."

The Princess hastened to do as she was instructed; the rock split from the top to the bottom: she entered with a victorious air the hall in which stood the three Princes with many others; she ran towards Cheri, who did not know her in her helmet and male attire, and could neither speak nor move. The green bird then told the Princess she must rub the eyes and mouth of all those she wished to disenchant with the red feather, which good office she did to all.

The three Princes and Belle-Etoile hastened to present themselves to the King; and when Belle-Etoile showed her treasures, the little green bird told him that the Princes Petit-Soleil and Heureux and the Princess Belle-Etoile were his children, and that Prince Cheri was his nephew. Queen Blondine, who had mourned for them all these years, embraced them, and the wicked Queen-Mother and old Feintise were justly punished. And the King, who thought his nephew Cheri the handsomest man at Court, consented to his marriage with Belle-Etoile. And lastly, to make everyone happy, the King sent for the Corsair and his wife, who gladly came.

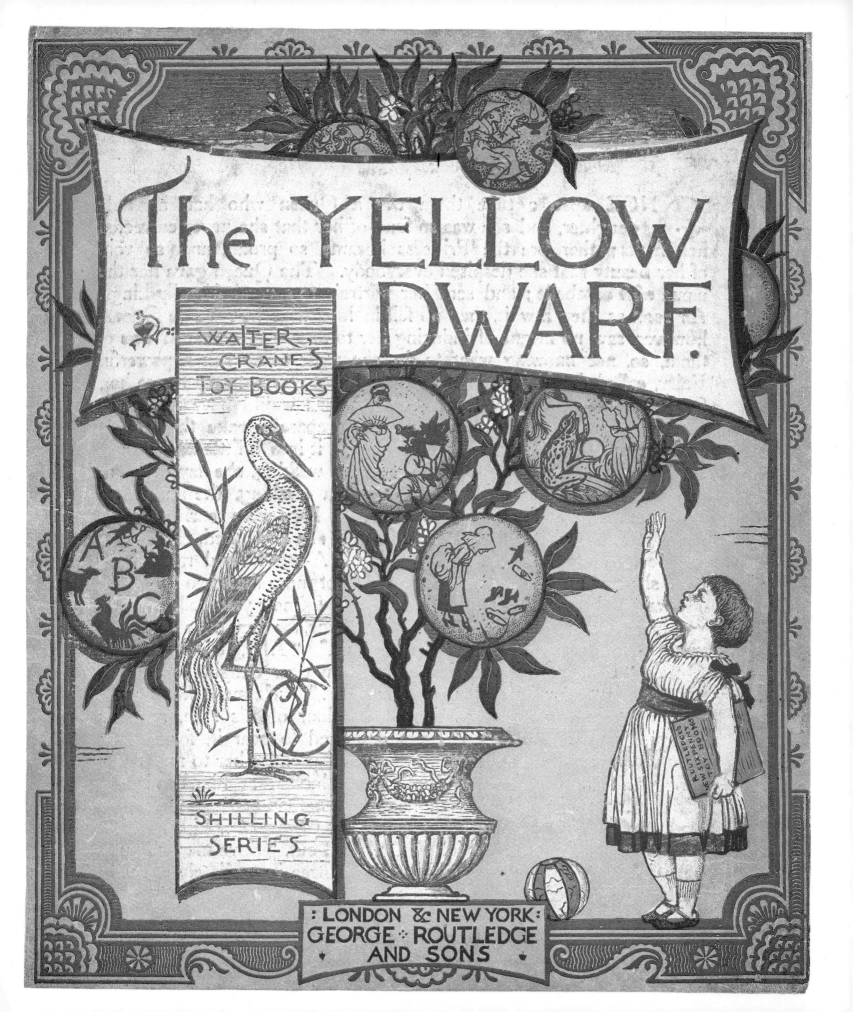

The YELLOW DWARF.

WALTER CRANE'S TOY BOOKS

SHILLING SERIES

: LONDON & NEW YORK :
GEORGE · ROUTLEDGE
AND SONS

THE YELLOW DWARF

ONCE upon a time there was a Queen who had an only daughter, and she was so fond of her that she never corrected her faults; therefore the Princess became so proud, and so vain of her beauty that she despised everybody. The Queen gave her the name of Toutebelle; and sent her portrait to several friendly kings. As soon as they saw it, they all fell in love with her. The Queen, however, saw no means of inducing her to decide in favour of one of them, so, not knowing what to do, she went to consult a powerful Fairy, called the Fairy of the Desert: but it was not easy to see her, for she was guarded by lions. The Queen would have had little chance if she had not known how to prepare a cake that would appease them. She made one herself, put it into a little basket, and set out on her journey. Being tired with walking, she lay down at the foot of a tree and fell asleep; and on awaking, she found her basket empty, and the cake gone, while the lions were roaring dreadfully. "Alas, what will become of me!" she exclaimed, clinging to the tree. Just then she heard, "Hist! A-hem!" and raising her eyes, she saw up in the tree a little man not more than two feet high. He was eating oranges, and said to her, "I know you well, Queen; you have good reason to be afraid of the lions, for they have devoured many before you, and—you have no cake." "Alas," cried the poor Queen, "I should die with less pain if my dear daughter were but married!" "How! you have a daughter!" exclaimed the Yellow Dwarf. (He was so called from the colour of his skin, and his living in an orange-tree.) "I am delighted to hear it, for I have sought a wife by land and sea. If you will promise her to me, I will save you from the lions." The Queen looked at him, and was scarcely less frightened at his horrible figure than at the lions. She made no answer until she saw them on the brow of a hill, running towards her. At this the poor Queen cried out, "Save me! Toutebelle is yours." The trunk of the orange-tree immediately opened; the Queen rushed into it; it closed, and the lions were baulked of their prey.

The unfortunate Queen then dropped insensible to the ground, and

while she was in this state she was transported to the palace, and placed in her own bed. When she awoke and recollected what had befallen her, she tried to persuade herself that it was all a dream and that she had never met with this dreadful adventure : but she fell into a melancholy state, so that she could scarcely speak, eat, or sleep.

The Princess, who loved her mother with all her heart, grew very uneasy. She often begged her to say what was the matter, but the Queen always put her off with some reason that the Princess saw plainly enough was not the real one. Being unable to control her anxiety, she resolved to seek the famous Fairy of the Desert, whose advice as to marrying she was also desirous of obtaining, for everybody pressed her to choose a husband. She took care to knead the cake herself, and pretending to go to bed early one evening, she went out by a back staircase, and thus, all alone, set out to find the Fairy. But on arriving at the orange-tree, she was seized with a desire to gather some of the fruit. She set down her basket and plucked some oranges ; but when she looked again for it, it had disappeared. Alarmed and distressed, she suddenly saw beside her the frightful little Dwarf. "What ails you, fair maid ?" said he. "Alas !" replied she, "I have lost the cake which was so necessary to insure my safe arrival at the abode of the Desert Fairy." "And what do you want with her ?" said the Dwarf. "I am her kinsman, and as clever as she is." "The Queen, my mother," replied the Princess, "has lately fallen into despair. I fancy I am the cause of it ; for she wishes me to marry ; but I have not yet seen any one I think worthy of me. It is for this reason I would consult the Fairy." "Don't give yourself that trouble, Princess," said the Dwarf ; "I can advise you better than she. The Queen is sorry that she has promised you in marriage." "The Queen promised me !" cried the Princess. "Oh, you must be mistaken." "Beautiful Princess," said the Dwarf, flinging himself at her feet, "it is I who am destined to enjoy such happiness." "My mother have you for her son-in-law !" exclaimed Toutebelle, recoiling ; "was there ever such madness !" "I care very little about the honour," said the Dwarf, angrily. "Here come the lions ; in three bites they will avenge me." At the same moment the poor Princess heard the roars of the savage beasts. "What will become of me ?" she cried. The Dwarf looked at her, and laughed contemptuously. "Be not angry," said the Princess ; "I would rather marry all the dwarfs in the world than perish in so frightful a manner." 'Look at me well, Princess, before you give me your word," replied he. "I have looked at you more than enough," said she. "The lions are approaching; save me!" She had scarcely uttered these words, when she fainted. On recovering, she found herself in her own bed, and on her finger a little ring made of a single red hair, which fitted her so closely that the skin might have been taken off sooner than the ring. When the Princess saw these things, and remembered what had taken place, she became very despondent, which pained the whole Court.

Toutebelle had now lost much of her pride. She saw no better way of getting out of her trouble than by marrying some great king with whom the Dwarf would not dare to dispute. She, therefore, consented to marry the King of the Gold Mines, a very powerful and handsome Prince, who loved her passionately. It is easy to imagine his joy when he received this news. Everything was prepared for one of the grandest entertainments that had ever been given. The King of the Gold Mines sent home for such sums of money that the sea was covered with the ships which brought them. Now that she had accepted him, the Princess found in the young King so much merit that she soon began to return his affection, and became very warmly attached to him.

At length the day so long wished for arrived. Everything being ready for the marriage, the people flocked in crowds to the great square in front of the palace. The Queen and Princess were advancing to meet the King, when they saw two large turkey-cocks, drawing a strange-looking box. Behind them came a tall old woman, whose age and decrepitude were no less remarkable than her ugliness. She leaned on a crutch. She wore a black ruff, a red hood, and a gown all in tatters. She took three turns round the gallery with her turkey-cocks before she spoke a word; then, stopping and brandishing her crutch, she cried, "Ho! ho! Queen!—Ho! ho! Princess! Do you fancy you can break your promises to my friend the Yellow Dwarf! I am the Fairy of the Desert! But for him and his orange-tree, know you not that my great lions would have devoured you?" "Ah! Princess," exclaimed the Queen, bursting into tears, "what promise have you made?" "Ah! Mother," cried Toutebelle, sorrowfully, "what promise have *you* made?" The King of the Gold Mines, enraged at this interruption, advanced upon the old woman, sword in hand, and cried, " Quit this palace for ever, or with thy life thou shalt atone for thy malice!"

Scarcely had he said this when the lid of the box flew up as high as the ceiling, with a terrific noise, and out of it issued the Yellow Dwarf, mounted on a large Spanish cat, who placed himself between the Fairy of the Desert and the King of the Gold Mines. " Rash youth!" cried he, " think not of assaulting this illustrious Fairy: it is with me alone thou hast to do! The faithless Princess who would give thee her hand has plighted her troth to me, and received mine. Look if she have not on her finger a ring of my hair." "Miserable monster," said the King to him, " hast thou the audacity to declare thyself the lover of this divine Princess?" The Yellow Dwarf struck his spurs into the sides of his cat, which set up a terrific squalling, and frightened everybody but the King, who pressed the Dwarf so closely that he drew a cutlass, and defying him to single combat, descended into the court-yard, the enraged King following him. Scarcely had they confronted each other, the whole Court being in the balconies to witness the combat, when the sun became as red as blood, and it grew so dark that they could scarcely see themselves. The two turkey-cocks appeared at the side of the Yellow Dwarf, casting out flames from their mouths and eyes. All these horrors did not shake the heart of the young King; but his courage failed when he saw the Fairy of the Desert, mounted upon a winged griffin, and armed with a lance, rush upon his dear Princess, and strike so fierce a blow that she fell into the Queen's arms bathed in her own blood. The King ran to rescue the Princess; but the Yellow Dwarf was too quick for him: he leaped with his cat into the balcony, snatched the Princess from the arms of the Queen, and disappeared with her.

The King was gazing in despair on this extraordinary scene, when he felt his eyesight fail; and by some irresistible power he was hurried through the air. The wicked Fairy of the Desert had no sooner set her eyes on him than her heart was touched by his charms. She bore him off to a cavern, where she loaded him with chains; and she hoped that the fear of death would make him forget Toutebelle. As soon as they had arrived there, she restored his sight, and appeared before him like a lovely nymph. "Can it be you, charming Prince?" she cried. "What misfortune has befallen you?" The King

replied, "Alas, fair nymph, I know not the object of the unkind Fairy who brought me hither." "Ah, my Lord," exclaimed the nymph, "if you are in the power of that woman you will not escape without marrying her." Whilst she thus pretended to take great interest in the King's affliction, he caught sight of her feet, which were like those of a griffin, and by this at once knew her to be the wicked Fairy. He, however, took no notice of it. "I do not," said he, "entertain any dislike to the Fairy of the Desert, but I cannot endure that she should keep me in chains like a criminal." The Fairy of the Desert, deceived by these words, resolved to carry the King to a beautiful spot. So she made him enter her chariot, to which she had now harnessed swans, and fled with him from one pole to the other.

Whilst thus travelling through the air, he beheld his dear Princess in a castle all of steel, the walls of which, reflecting the rays of the sun, became like burning-glasses, and scorched to death all who ventured to approach them. She was reclining on the bank of a stream. As she lifted her eyes, she saw the King pass by with the Fairy of the Desert, who, through her magic arts, seemed to be very beautiful; and this made her more unhappy than ever, as she thought the King was untrue to her. She thus became jealous, and was offended with the poor King, while he was in great grief at being so rapidly borne away from her.

At length they reached a meadow, covered with a thousand various flowers. A deep river surrounded it, and in the distance arose a superb palace. As soon as the swans had descended, the Fairy of the Desert led the King into a handsome apartment, and did all she could that he might not think himself actually a prisoner.

The King, who had his reasons for saying kind things to the old Fairy, was not sparing of them, and by degrees obtained leave to walk by the sea-side. One day he heard a voice, and looking rapidly around him, he saw a female of great beauty, whose form terminated in a long fish's tail. As soon as she was near enough to speak to him, she said, "I know the sad state to which you are reduced by the loss of your Princess; if you are willing, I will convey you from this fatal spot." As the King hesitated, the Syren said, "Do not think I am laying a snare for you; if you will confide in me, I will save you." "I have such perfect confidence in you," said the King, "that I will do whatever you command." "Come with me then," said the

The Yellow Dwarf.

Syren; "I will first leave on the shore a figure so perfectly resembling you that it shall deceive the Fairy, and then convey you to the Steel Castle."

She cut some sea-rushes, and, making a large bundle of them, they became so like the King of the Gold Mines that he had never seen so astonishing a change. The friendly Syren then made the King seat himself upon her great fish's tail, and carried him off. They soon arrived at the Steel Castle. The side that faced the sea was the only part of it that the Yellow Dwarf had left open. The Syren told the King that he would find Toutebelle by the stream near which he had seen her when he passed over with the Fairy. But as he would have to contend with some enemies before he could reach her, she gave him a diamond sword, with which he could face the greatest danger, warning him *never to let it fall*. The King thanked the Syren warmly, and strode on rapidly towards the Steel Castle. Before he had gone far four terrible sphinxes surrounded him, and would quickly have torn him in pieces, if the diamond sword had not proved as useful to him as the Syren had predicted. He dealt each of them its death-blow, then advancing again, he met six dragons, covered with scales. But his courage remained unshaken, and making good use of his sword, there was not one that he did not cut in half at a blow. Without further obstacle, he entered the grove in which he had seen Toutebelle. She was seated beside the fountain, pale and suffering. At first she indignantly fled from him. "Do not condemn me unheard," said he. "I am an unhappy lover, who has been compelled, despite himself, to offend you." He flung himself at her feet, but in so doing he unfortunately let fall the sword. The Yellow Dwarf, who had lain hidden behind a shrub, no sooner saw it out of the King's hands than he sprang forward to seize it. The Princess uttered a loud shriek, which luckily caused the King to turn suddenly round, just in time to snatch up the sword. With one blow he slew the wicked Dwarf, and then conducted the Princess to the sea-shore, where the friendly Syren was waiting to convey them to the Queen. On their arrival at the palace, the wedding took place, and Toutebelle, cured of her vanity, lived happily with the King of the Gold Mines.